www.gwpublishing.com

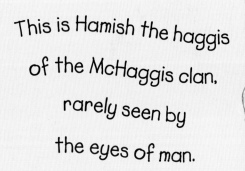

Hamish

This is Hamish the haggis
of the McHaggis clan,
rarely seen by
the eyes of man.

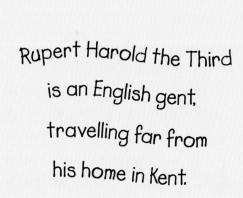

Rupert

Rupert Harold the Third
is an English gent,
travelling far from
his home in Kent.

Our Jeannie's an osprey with wide sweeping wings,
who is easily distracted by all sorts of things.

Jeannie

Angus

Young Angus is cheeky and likes playing the fool,
whatever he's doing he's got to look cool.

For Abigail and Ruaridh
with love. L.S.

For Chris, my son-in-law
with love. S.J.C.

www.lindastrachan.com
www.hamishmchaggis.com

First published in paperback in Great Britain 2012

Designed by Mark Dyment

Printed in China

Published by

GW Publishing
PO Box 15070
Dunblane
FK15 5AN

www.gwpublishing.com

ISBN 978-0-9570844-0-7

Hamish McHaggis

and
The Great
Glasgow Treasure Hunt

By Linda Strachan
Illustrated by Sally J. Collins

One sunny morning Hamish McHaggis was packing the Whirry Bang when Angus came whizzing by on his skateboard.

"Where are you going, Hamish?" asked Angus. "Where's Jeannie?"
"She's gone to visit Maggie the fox." Hamish pushed a large bag
into the back of the Whirry Bang. "And we're off to Glasgow
to meet her, too."
"Can I come? Can I? Can I?" Angus jumped off his
skateboard.
"Of course you can," Rupert grinned at him.

Whizz

"You'll need to be ready in two minutes," Hamish said.
"I'll be ready in one minute flat!"
Angus raced off and, a moment later, he tossed his backpack
into the Whirry Bang and they set off for Glasgow.

They soon arrived at Pollok Park.
"Dearie me, Maggie, what's wrong?"
Hamish asked.
"Oh, it's the bairns. They've run off, again.
They're pure gallus!"

"She means her wee cubs,"
Jeannie told Rupert. "They're always getting into trouble."
"I've got to find them," Maggie fussed. "But I need to make up
clues for the Great Glasgow Treasure Hunt. It's today!"

"Could we help?" asked Angus.

"Maybe," said Maggie. "On this Treasure Hunt people are given a list of clues and have to visit different places to find the answers. But someone has to make up the clues first!"

"We'll make up clues for you, Maggie," Hamish said. "Dinna fash yersel. Just you go and find your cubs."

"You're magic, Hamish!" Maggie looked happier already. "I've marked some places on this map where you can get ideas for clues."

"I've got an idea for the first one." Hamish had a smug smile.

"What is it? What is it?" Angus was so excited he jumped up onto the fence.

"The clue could be ...

What's the name of Jock and Ellie's baby?

"And draw a picture," suggested Jeannie.

"That's easy!" Angus patted the little Highland calf. "It's Abigail!
Let's go inside Pollok House and see if we can find another clue."

It's Abigail!

Jeannie flew up above their heads.
"I think I've found a clue, Hamish," she squawked.

A golden dragon curls above your head. Can you see what's in her arms?

"I can't see a dragon." Angus moaned.

"Mmm, above your head," muttered Hamish. "Ah, yes."

Angus looked up. "Yippee! I see it," he said. "It's an egg."

Hamish rubbed his tummy. "I'm hungry! I think it's time for a picnic."

"Not yet, Hamish," Jeannie shook her head. "We've got to think up more clues."

"Let's go to Riverside Museum in the Whirry Bang." Rupert showed them his leaflet. "It's got cars, ships and trains. You'd enjoy it, Hamish."

"Angus and I could get out at Kelvingrove Museum," Jeannie suggested "Let's meet there for our picnic."

Rumble

At Riverside Museum Rupert was fascinated by the huge trains and the fire engines, but Hamish stared at the cars on the walls.

"They seem to have almost every kind of transport here."

Rupert shook his head. "You know what they don't have, Hamish. **A Whirry Bang!**"

"Now, that would be braw," Hamish grinned. "I've just thought of a clue."

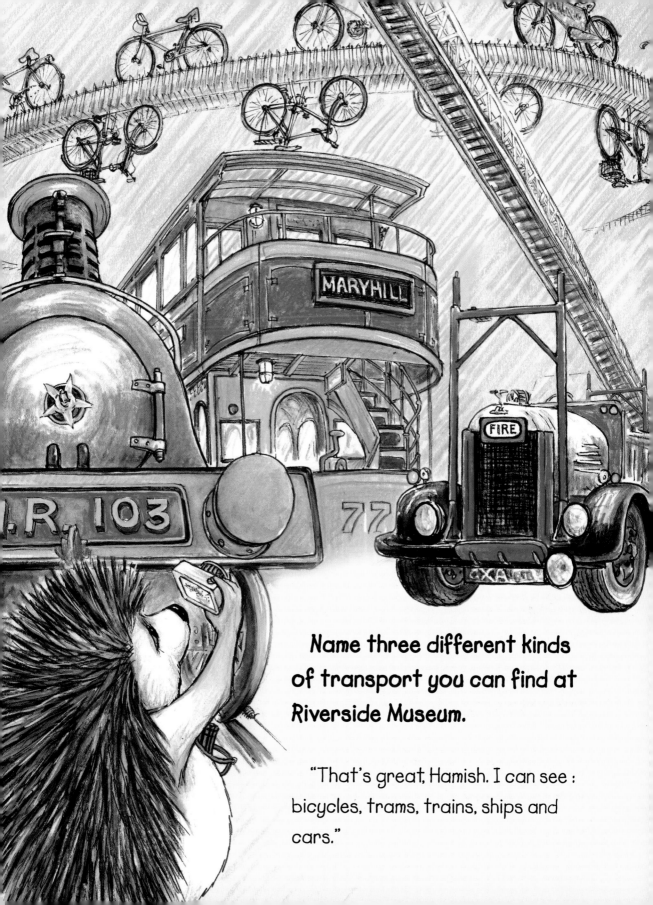

Name three different kinds of transport you can find at Riverside Museum.

"That's great, Hamish. I can see : bicycles, trams, trains, ships and cars."

"Come and see this, Rupert!"

Hamish was very excited. "It's a whole street. It must have looked like this years ago, when they used horses instead of cars."

"This street gives me an idea for another clue, Hamish."

Look in the Italian café, the saddlers and the chemist. Name something they sold in each one.

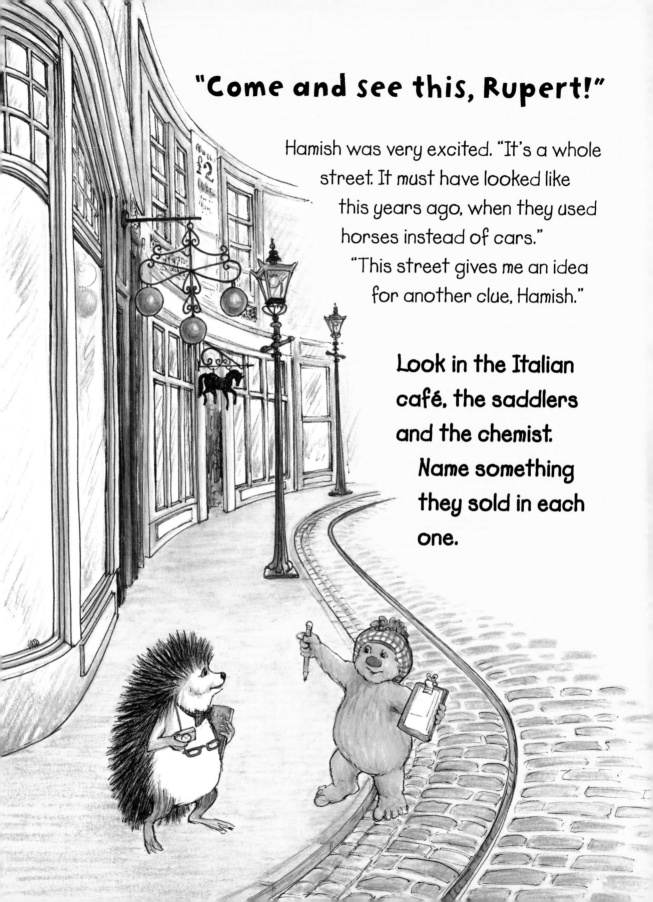

"Ah! Let me see," said Hamish. "In the Italian Café they sold **ice cream**, in the Saddlers it was **shoes**, and the Chemist shop sold **medicine**."

"That's right," said Rupert. "Now let's have a look outside."

They looked up at the tall windows of the museum building.
"Look, Rupert, you can see the reflection of the ship in the glass."
Rupert looked towards the quay. "The ship is called The Glenlee.
That could be our next clue."

What is the name of the Tall Ship?

Hamish nodded "That's a good idea, Rupert."
"You know, Hamish, I think I'd have been a
grand sailor." Rupert swayed from side to side.

"Oh, a life on the ocean waves,"

"But Rupert," Hamish tried not to laugh,
"you get seasick!"

Meanwhile at Kelvingrove Museum, Angus and Jeannie were having a wonderful time finding clues. "I've got one, Jeannie!" Angus was very pleased with himself.

Higher than a giraffe I fly, but I am not a bird. What am I?

"That's a fantastic clue, Angus. That plane is called a Spitfire," Jeannie told him.

Angus was looking up at the huge elephant. "What about this one, Jeannie?"

What is *Sir Roger*? He has tusks and a long nose. Draw his picture.

Jeannie didn't reply. "This is exactly how I see the world," she said, staring at the floor.
"What about...'

It's under your feet and helps you find your way around Glasgow. What is it?

"It's a map!" said Angus.

Jeannie was looking at a painting while Angus was busy drawing.

"Is that a clue, Angus?" Jeannie asked.

"Yes, it's called a pictogram, Jeannie," Angus explained. "That's because **the clue is in pictures and words.** It will tell you the name of the painting you are looking at"

"What a great idea, Angus. Let me see if I can work it out."

Jeannie looked at his drawings.

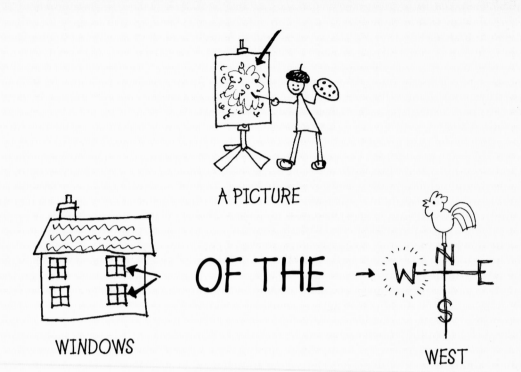

A PICTURE

OF THE

WINDOWS

WEST

"So, the answer is a picture called **Windows of the West!**" said Angus.

"Wow Jeannie!
Look over there!"

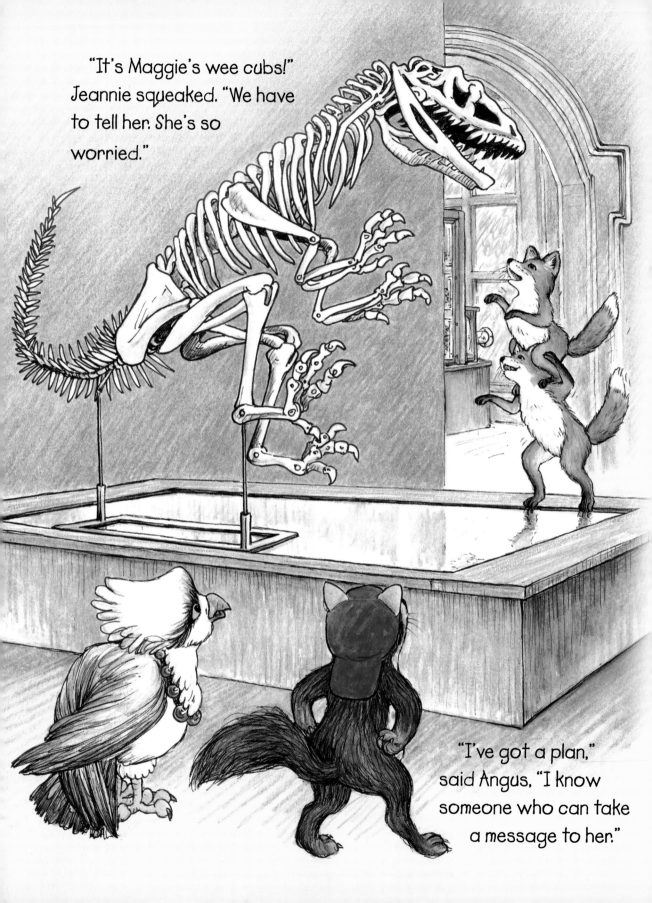

"It's Maggie's wee cubs!" Jeannie squeaked. "We have to tell her. She's so worried."

"I've got a plan," said Angus, "I know someone who can take a message to her."

He raced over to the beehive. "Hello, little buzzy friends. Can you do us a favour, please?"

"**Bzzzz**," said the bees. "How can we **buzz** about and help, Angus?"

"Can you find Maggie the fox and tell her we've found her cubs in the museum?"

"**Bzzzz**. We can do that!" The bees flew out into the summer sunshine.

When Hamish and Rupert arrived at
Kelvingrove Museum a few minutes later,
they could hear music. The huge organ
had started playing some merry tunes.

"There's Angus and Jeannie. And
look who's with them!"

Hamish looked up at the balcony.
"Well, fancy that! Maggie will be well
pleased that they've found her cubs."

Maggie arrived just in time for the start of the Treasure Hunt.

"Come and see the clues we found, Maggie," said Angus.

"These are amazing," she said. "I'm sure this will be the best Treasure Hunt ever. Thank you so much for finding my bairns, too."

"Maggie," Angus was so excited that he was hopping about, "can I go on the Treasure Hunt, too? Please? Please?"

Hamish laughed. "Oh no, Angus. You know all the answers. It wouldn't be fair. But we can have a picnic instead, and perhaps we can join in when you have another Treasure Hunt, Maggie?"

"Of course," Maggie agreed.
"You can come along next year!"

Clues:

At Pollok Park and Pollok House

1. What's the name of Jock and Ellie's baby? Draw a picture.
2. A golden dragon curls above your head. Can you see what's in her arms?

At Riverside Museum

3. Name three different kinds of transport you can find at Riverside Museum.
4. Look in the Italian café, the saddlers and the chemist. Name something they sold in each one.
5. What is the name of the Tall Ship?

At Kelvingrove Museum

6. Higher than a giraffe I fly, but I am not a bird. What am I?
7. What is Sir Roger? He has tusks and a long nose. Draw his picture.
8. It's under your feet and helps you find your way around Glasgow. What is it?
9. Pictogram: picture clues.

Answers:

9. Windows of the West a painting.
8. A map.
7. An elephant plus a drawing.
6. A plane (a Spitfire).
5. The Glenlee.
4. The Italian Café: food, drink, ice cream. The Saddlers: shoes and leather goods; The Chemist: medicines.
3. Bike, car, tram, ship, bus, fire engine, train, van.
2. An egg.
1. Abigail, and a drawing of a Highland calf.

DID YOU KNOW?

Coorie Doon means to nestle or cosy down comfortably.

Braw means good.

The bairns means the children.

Dinna Fash Yersel means don't worry or fuss.

You're magic means you're great or amazing.

Pure gallus means to be daring, cheeky or a bit wild.

Haggis It is commonly thought that a Haggis has three legs, two long and one short. Hamish thinks this is plain silly.

**Hamish McHaggis
and The search for The
Loch Ness Monster**

978-0-9546701-5-3

**Hamish McHaggis
and The Edinburgh Adventure**

978-0-9546701-7-7

**Hamish McHaggis
and The Ghost of Glamis**

978-0-9546701-9-1

**Hamish McHaggis
and The Skye Surprise**

978-0-9546701-8-4

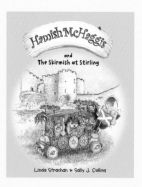

**Hamish McHaggis
and The Skirmish at Stirling**

978-0-9551564-1-0

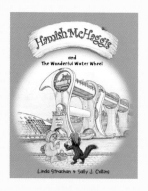

**Hamish McHaggis
and The Wonderful Water Wheel**

978-0-9551564-0-3

**Hamish McHaggis
and The Wonderful Water Wheel**

978-0-9554145-5-8

**Hamish McHaggis
and The Clan Gathering**

978-0-9561211-2-7

**Hamish McHaggis
and The Great
Glasgow Treasure Hunt**

978-0-9570844-0-7

**Hamish McHaggis
Activity and Story Book**

978-0-9554145-1-0

Also by the
same author
and illustrator

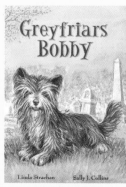

Greyfriars Bobby

978-0-9551564-2-7